THE McCLURE FAMI[LY]

N

INDIANA

OHIO

Lawrenceburgh   • Cincinnati

Ohio River

Madison   •

Maysville °

KENTUCKY

Jeffersonville

• Louisville

NEY ON THE OHIO RIVER

Pittsburgh
Steubenville
PENNSYLVANIA

Wheeling

Marietta

Point Pleasant

VIRGINIA

Scott Russell Sanders

THE FLOATING HOUSE

Illustrated by *Helen Cogancherry*

ALADDIN PAPERBACKS

First Aladdin Paperbacks edition December 1999

Aladdin Paperbacks
An imprint of Simon & Schuster Children's Publishing Division
1230 Avenue of the Americas
New York, NY 10020

Book design by Julie Quan
The text for this book was set in 16 pt. Berkeley O.S.
The illustrations were done in watercolor, with pencil highlights.

Printed in Hong Kong
2 4 6 8 10 9 7 5 3 1

The Library of Congress has cataloged the hardcover edition as follows:
Sanders, Scott R. (Scott Russell)
The floating house / by Scott Russell Sanders ; illustrated by
Helen Cogancherry.—1st ed.
p.   cm.
Summary: In 1815, the McClures sail their flatboat from Pittsburgh
down the Ohio River and settle in what would later become Indiana.
ISBN 0-02-778137-2 (hc.)
[1. Rivers—Fiction. 2. Flatboats—Fiction. 3. Frontier and pioneer life—Fiction.]
1. Cogancherry, Helen, ill. II. Title.
PZ7.S19786F1 1995
[Fic]—dc20   94-15277
ISBN 0-689-83049-1 (Aladdin pbk.)

∽ ∽ ∽

To Deryl Dale, for his carpentry and singing
To Linda Chapman, for her gardening
To their children, Anna and Macey, for joyously growing
    —S. R. S.

With love to my son, Mike, and
his wife, Sue, who have the pioneer spirit
    —H. C.

∽ ∽ ∽

The winter of 1815 was so cold, the Ohio River froze from shore to shore. Wayne and Birdy McClure and their two children, Mary and Jonathan, huddled in the cabin of their flatboat, wrapped in quilts, listening to the ice groan and creak like the stairs in an old house.

Their boat still rested on dry land in Pittsburgh, along with hundreds of other flatboats, keelboats, skiffs and scows, canoes and barges and rafts, even a few of the newfangled steamboats, all waiting for the spring thaw to open the river.

Then one morning after a week of sunshine, the McClures woke to a sound like thunder. They looked out to see the green ice cracked into slabs, and black water showing through.

"Look," Mary cried. "The river's yawning!"

"Sleepy old river," said Jonathan.

The current soon swept the river clear. Everybody started launching boats, one family helping another. Those looking for new land, like the McClures, were eager to reach the wild country downstream, where you could buy farms for a dollar an acre and where the dirt was so rich, people said, you could plant a stick and it would break out in leaves.

In a crowd of boats, the McClures set off.

The swifter boats pulled away, leaving the McClures to drift in company with a few other families.

Mr. McClure balanced on the cabin roof and steered with a long sweeping oar. Mrs. McClure read aloud from *The Navigator,* a book of advice for travelers on the Ohio. The horse, the cow, the mule, and the pig rode behind the cabin, munching corn, thumping the deck. The children rode up front with the wagon and plow, among barrels, bundles, and tools. Mary and Jonathan were a little afraid to feel the boat rocking, but they were also excited to be riding the great river at last. Their job was to watch for sandbars and snags, and to give a holler if they saw danger ahead.

Despite their hollering, sometimes the flatboat struck a soggy stump or scraped a rock, and sometimes it grounded on gravel or sand.

When that happened, Mr. and Mrs. McClure would wade in the shallows and shove with poles, and other travelers would lend a hand until the boat slid free.

Every bump made the horse whinny and prance. From inside the cabin, Mary and Jonathan sang funny songs to calm him.

By day they floated lazily downstream, about the speed of a person walking. If the morning was foggy, Mr. McClure judged the distance to shore by throwing stones and listening for a splash or thud. If they met a steamboat chugging upriver, or a keelboat gliding along with its crew of grunting men, Mary blew hard on the tin horn, and Jonathan yelled, "Flatboat coming!"

Every afternoon before sunset, the McClures tied up on the bank, along with four or five other boats. The children pulled in trotlines to see what fish they had caught, and they gathered driftwood for fires. They refilled water barrels from the river, but let the mud settle out before drinking. The mothers traded food and lantern oil and stories. The fathers hunted deer and turkey for supper, then took turns all night standing guard.

Before falling asleep, Mary and Jonathan watched embers glowing in the sandbox on deck. They smelled sawdust from the poplar and walnut lumber their father had used in building the boat, and the tar he had used for caulking the joints. They smelled tallow from the candles their mother had made. They listened to owls hoot and wolves howl. Even on windless nights, they heard limbs crashing in the woods. And always, beneath every other sound, they heard the lap and stir of the river.

The farther they journeyed, the wilder the land appeared. There were clearings for homesteads, and occasional towns, but mostly the shores were thick with trees, still brown and bare from the hard winter. Grapevines looped from trunk to trunk, and nests clotted the branches. Eagles and hawks circled overhead.

Bears swam across the current, snorting, black eyes gleaming. And once the whole river was blocked by a churning carpet of squirrels.

As the flatboat glided along, people called from shore, "Hello, the boat!"

"Hello, the shore!" the children called back. "What place is this?"

Steubenville, the people might answer, or Wheeling, Marietta, Point Pleasant, Gallipolis, Maysville. So many mysterious names! Jonathan and Mary had never before set foot outside of Pennsylvania, and here within a month they would see Ohio and western Virginia, Kentucky, and Indiana. Why, Indiana wasn't even a state yet, it was so thinly settled. And that was where they were headed, to a settlement named Jeffersonville, across the river from Louisville, at the falls of the Ohio.

"How will we know the place?" the children asked.

"You'll hear the roar of the rapids," their mother said.

"How long until we get there?" they kept asking.

A good while, their father answered; then he said a week; then only a few days.

§ § §

The children listened for a waterfall. They studied every island, every bluff, every field planted with spindly orchards, every log cabin surrounded by stumps.

Would the house they built in Indiana look like one of those lonesome cabins?

Just when it seemed they had reached the edge of the world, they came to Cincinnati, a city as large as Pittsburgh, all chimneys and church spires. The wharves were crowded with ships. The streets rang with hammers, clattered with carts, huffed and puffed with steam engines.

§   §   §

They floated on, past settlements with names like Lawrenceburgh and Madison. At last, one day about noon, Mary and Jonathan heard a low rumble, like the sound of an empty barrel rolling on the floor. They stared ahead and saw the water foaming white. "Rocks!" they shouted.

"Those must be the falls," their father said.

"And that must be Louisville," their mother said, pointing to a sizable town on the left bank.

"So that must be Jeffersonville," their father said, steering the boat toward a village on the right bank.

No sooner had the McClures tied up at the dock than dogs came running to sniff them and children came running to meet them and folks of all ages came to help unload the flatboat.

From the government office, the McClures bought a parcel of land overlooking the falls. Before dark, with more help from these new neighbors, they dismantled the boat, hauled the lumber to their farm, and began building a house with the very same wood.

Back again on dry land, Mary and Jonathan could still hear the river. It poured through their minds, waking and sleeping. Sometimes on windy nights when the rapids were roaring, the children imagined their house might lift from its foundation, slide down the bank, and go riding the river once more, heading downstream to unknown places.